Sutherland House
Episode One
"Andover"

David R. Beshears

Large Print Edition

Greybeard Publishing
Washington State

Greybeard Publishing
P.O. Box 480
McCleary, WA 98557-0480

ISBN 978-1-947231-12-2

Sutherland House
Episode One
"Andover"

Prolog

Sharon stood in the center of the forest clearing, bright moonlight shining down upon her. She was attractive, with long brown hair, was wearing a long, flowing white dress.

A dozen men and women stood along the perimeter of the clearing, half hidden in the shadows of the surrounding fir trees. They were dressed in contemporary street clothes, some loose fitting and fluttering in a slight breeze.

They were looking in at the forty year old woman dressed in white. They showed no emotion.

Sharon looked frightened. She turned slowly about. Those standing in the shadows continued to look into the center of the clearing, their focus on Sharon growing steadier, more determined, yet with no passion.

A woman slowly laid her head back, closed her eyes.

A second observer laid his head back and closed his eyes.

Sharon continued to spin slowly about, looking to those in the half-shadow with increasing desperation. Her long hair fluttered and flowed, caught in the twisting breeze that grew steadily stronger.

A cloud drifted in front of the silver moon and the night grew dark. Shadows pushed into the clearing from the black of the forest.

Chapter One

Matthew Sutherland drove his twenty year old Lincoln slowly through the automated gates of the Sutherland House estate, up the wandering drive through the estate grounds and toward the house itself.

Matthew looked to be about forty, but his eyes revealed that he had seen much more than four decades. He had a kind face. He wore the black armband of mourning.

The estate grounds were a mix of different styles, with a variety of shrubs, plants, walks and short garden walls, as if it had all been put together piecemeal over many years as moods changed and as the gardener discovered new things and came up with new ideas; all of which were true.

The two-storey house itself was modest and surprisingly small considering the expansive grounds and high walls that surrounded it. It was unpretentious, while at the same time stately.

Matthew came into the front foyer and tossed his keys into a dish on a small table beside the front door, walked into the living room. The house was clean and comfortable; the furniture quality without being ostentatious, a mix of styles and periods, collected over the span of many years.

He dropped down onto the couch, slid back and tiredly rubbed at his face. He struggled to hold onto his emotions, fighting back grief. He wasn't ready to give into it.

He sat up then, leaned forward, elbows on his knees. He looked around him at the home that he had shared with Sharon for so many years.

It all threatened to fall in on him.

He ignored the sound of the front door opening and closing. Moments later, Jennifer Sutherland came into the room from the foyer. She moved quickly to the easy chair and sat, stared at Matthew. She looked a bit irritated with her father.

She was twenty, attractive in a very natural way, being that there was nothing artificial in her looks or her manner. She was wearing a full black dress and shawl.

"You can't just walk out like that," she said. Yes. Definitely irritated, but restrained.

"Sure I can."

"No. You can't."

Matthew turned to face his daughter, his gaze lost.

"You learn that in college, did you?"

"That's rude. It was rude."

"Yeah." Matthew slid back in the couch, laid his head back and stared up at the ceiling. "I wonder if the panels are shrinking or the house is settling."

"Dad—" Jennifer tried her best to ignore the ceiling.

"Do you see that?" He asked. "There's a gap between two of the panels."

"It's been there since I was three," said Jennifer, without looking up.

Matthew brought his head forward again, straightened with a sigh. He wore a studious frown.

"School break must be about over," he said. "When do you head back?"

"I told you. I've taken leave. Jorgenson said that I can pick it up again whenever I'm ready."

"Jorgenson thinks he owes us something."

"He does owe us something."

Matthew rubbed his face again, sighed.

"You shouldn't have done that, Jen. You don't want to fall behind."

"Don't worry about that, Dad. I'll be fine."

"This is your senior year."

"I'm fine."

Matthew stared at Jennifer for a long moment, then turned away. He stared absently up at the ceiling, at the gap between two of the panels.

"What a crappy day."

Jennifer leaned forward, rested her elbows on her knees. She looked carefully at her father. She appeared about to cry, pushed it back.

"I love you, Dad."

The room fell silent; the house was suddenly very empty.

"I guess it's you and me now, Jen," said Matthew.

Jennifer stood then and went over to her father. She sat beside him. They held onto each other.

"We'll be all right," she said, consoling.

"I know," he managed to say. "I know."

§

Matthew took the narrow stairs down to the basement. To one side were free-standing shelves filled with neatly labeled home-canned jars of fruits and vegetables. The other side of the basement contained a small workshop. There was a workbench with a set of shelves beside it.

Matthew reached into the set of shelves and released a hidden latch. There was a metallic click. The shelves swung open, gliding easily, revealing a shaft with a ladder leading down.

He stepped into the shaft, onto the ladder, started down.

He climbed off the ladder and into "the Apartment". The lights came on automatically as he walked into the room.

The Apartment was comfortable contemporary, high-tech mixed with the every day. There was an opening in the wall behind him with the shaft leading up to the main house. On either side of the shaft opening were built-in shelves filled with books. A door along the wall to Matthew's right led to the armory, another to the bathroom. There was a counter beyond, behind which was a small kitchen.

Set into the wall on Matthew's left was a large viewing screen, beside that a bank of computer monitors, five across and four rows high.

A door in the far wall opened to a long hallway leading to an underground garage. To the left of the door were racks of computer network, server and communications equipment. Beside these was a computer station with desk and chair.

There was a living area in the center of "The Apartment", with couch and chair, a round kitchen table and chairs.

Matthew took off his jacket and tossed it onto the couch, revealing that he was wearing a shoulder holster and weapon. He walked across the room to the armory closet as he slipped out of the holster. A mix of sophisticated weaponry and standard weapons were mounted on one wall of the closet. He hung up his holster, unloaded and set the pistol into its slot.

He came out of the armory and went into the small bathroom. He spoke as he washed his hands and face.

"Computer," he said, impassively.

"Yes, Matthew?" came from hidden speakers. The computer voice sounded almost human, but with a lack of true emotion behind the words and an almost too perfect quality to the syntax and pronunciation.

Computer did strive, however, to inject familiarity into the conversations that it held with Matthew and Jennifer, previously with Sharon.

Matthew quickly dried his hands and returned to the main room, started into the kitchen.

"Anything more on Sharon's death since your last report?" he asked.

"All three regional newspapers carried the obituary," stated

Computer. "No additional articles. No newspapers outside the local area contain any reference. There has been no mention of Sharon Sutherland in any monitored television broadcast, radio broadcast or Internet news feeds.

Matthew took a can of iced tea out of the refrigerator and returned to the main area.

"Items of interest," he requested flatly.

"Forty-eight items identified for your review."

Matthew frowned, moved slowly to the couch. He sat down, opened the can of iced tea.

"Any that could possibly relate to Sharon's death?"

"No possible connections identified."

"Are any of the items Red Priority?"

"I have identified six items identified as Red Priority."

Matthew hesitated, absently rubbed at his temple.

"Not now." He stretched out on the couch, set the can on the floor. "Dim lights."

The lights dimmed, leaving only a faint glow in the room. Tiny red indicator lights inset into the computer equipment all about the room occasionally flickered.

Matthew rolled onto his side and immediately fell asleep.

Jennifer stood over her father, asleep on the couch. She placed a hand on his shoulder. He woke, sat up.

"Good morning," she said.

"'morning..." he looked curiously at the blanket that had been

covering him, set it aside.
"Morning?"

Jennifer turned away and started toward the kitchen. She obviously knew her way around the Apartment.

"I'll bet you're hungry," she said.

"A bit."

Jennifer began rummaging about cabinets and the refrigerator.

"I'll fix us something while you get cleaned up."

Matthew mumbled unintelligibly on his way to the bathroom.

Jennifer began cutting up fruit. She heard the shower running.

"Computer?" she asked.

"Hello, Jennifer," came the voice of Computer. "I am pleased to hear your voice. I have missed you."

"Thank you, Computer. I've missed you, too,"

"How is your education coming?"

"I have no doubt that you know exactly how I am doing."

"Grades are not fully representative of how someone is doing, Jennifer."

Jennifer smiled, put the plate of fruit on the counter.

"I'm doing fine," she said.

"I am pleased to hear that," said Computer.

"Anything new on Mom's murder?"

"No, Jennifer. I am sorry."

"Thank you."

There was a long pause then. The only sounds came from the running computer equipment and the low thrum of the running shower.

"I liked your mother very much," said Computer.

"Me too, Computer," said Jennifer.

Chapter Two

Jennifer was standing in the kitchen, opposite Matthew sitting at the counter. They were eating a breakfast of fruit and toast, with juice. Matthew was dressed comfortably, refreshed after his shower.

"Nothing new on Mom," said Jennifer.

Matthew only nodded, continued eating.

"Dad, I've been thinking." Jennifer started then, cautiously. "I think I should come into the business right away."

Matthew put down his fork, a chunk of cantaloupe still speared, and picked up his glass of juice.

"You need to finish school," he said. He took a drink.

"I can help you."

"No." Another swallow of juice.

"I was going to join you and Mom soon enough anyway."

"Things have changed."

"They certainly have," she said.

Matthew stared down at his glass, fought a number of emotions, all of which threatened to show themselves on his stone face.

"You coming into the family business... it wasn't supposed to—"

"I understand that, Dad. I do." Jennifer started to reach a hand across the counter, pulled it back. "You can't do this alone."

"Jen..." Matthew let the thought fade.

One of the red indicator lights beneath the monitor set into the wall next to the counter began to flash. A small label under the light read 'Main Gate'.

A moment later the monitor activated. It showed a young man, about twenty years old, standing near the communication box at the gate. He had the look and manner of the kid next door.

"It's Sam," groaned Jennifer.

"I doubt he's here to see me," said Matthew.

"Computer… activate," said Jennifer, her tone surrendering. "Hello, Sam."

"Jennifer," said Sam, leaning nearer the communication box. His voice sounded tinny coming through the speaker. "I wanted to make sure you were all right."

"I'm fine, Sam."

"When your dad left like that... and then you—"

"We're okay, Sam. I'm sorry we ran out."

"No!" Sam said quickly. "That's all right. Everyone understood."

There was a long pause. Sam looked about, looked to the camera.

"Are you going to let me in?" he asked then.

Jennifer looked irritably over at Matthew, who had miraculously regained his appetite and was busily finishing up the fruit.

"Sure," she sighed. "Computer, monitor off."

The monitor went blank. Jennifer pushed away from the counter and started out of the kitchen.

"Main gate open," she said, starting toward the ladder.

"Thanks for breakfast," said Matthew, his focus across the counter, as he picked up his juice glass. "You kids have fun."

"And another thing, Dad," she said, climbing onto the ladder. "A ladder? A lousy ladder?"

She disappeared into the shaft. The sound of her voice became muffled, only her legs visible.

"All the money spent putting this place together, and you couldn't spring for an elevator?"

Matthew's smile came and faded. He pushed away from the counter, walked around and into the kitchen. He put the breakfast dishes into the dishwasher, cleaned the counter. He drifted into the center of main room and stood behind the couch. He looked at the rows of inactive monitors, then at the large wall display, currently dark.

"Computer," he said.

"Yes, Matthew?"

Matthew stared dully at the wall.

"Nothing," he said.

Matthew felt very, very alone.

The Academy grounds were eerily empty of people, despite it being mid-afternoon, the day sunny and warm. There were several old, stately buildings of brick and ivy. The grounds themselves were green lawns and wide, winding walkways. Several hundred feet from the main building stood a large, ancient oak tree, hovering over a wide walkway running from the small parking lot to the main administration building.

A nine year old girl was standing in the window of her room in the dormitory, looking out at the grounds and the large oak tree. Mary's face was reflected in the glass. The quarters behind her were small; a single narrow bed, a desk and chair; there was a door to the closet, a larger door leading out to the hall.

Mary continued to look contemplatively outside. There was a sadness about her.

She lifted her gaze slightly. Despite the fact that there could be no breeze, her hair began to flutter.

She closed her eyes.

Her hair brushed back from her face against a breeze that did not exist.

§

The lights of the Apartment had gone dim. Matthew was standing behind the couch, looking across the room at the far wall. He slowly turned his head, lifted his gaze and looked up and to one side.

There was something...

He sensed... something.

Chapter Three

Jennifer stepped off the ladder and into the Apartment. The lights were on. Several of the monitors in the far wall were on, displaying nebulous scenes from security cameras located in unremarkable office buildings.

"Computer, where's Dad?" she asked.

"Matthew is in the garage, Jennifer."

Jennifer walked across the room and opened the door in the opposite wall. She entered a long, narrow hallway, lit by several ceiling light panels evenly spaced along the hall.

She opened the door at the far end of the hall and walked into the underground garage.

It looked much like an auto service center. Along the left side were six stalls containing an assortment of vehicles: a 64 Comet, an old Bronco, a small converted school bus, a late model BMW, a 97 Ford pickup, a pair of dirt bikes, and a Harley-Davidson Sportser.

On the right was a line of service bays; a chest-high counter spanned the length of the wall.

At the far end, an opening to a tunnel that curved away and out of sight.

Jennifer moved along the line of vehicles until she found Matthew under the hood of the immaculate 1964 Mercury Comet.

"Dad?"

Matthew answered from under the hood: "Yeah."

"Dad, what are you doing?" She sounded disheartened.

"I'm walking the dog."

"Dad…"

"Jennifer, I'm working on the car." He continued to speak from under the hood. "The car needs work—I'm working on it."

Jennifer watched Matthew work for several seconds before trying again.

"Listen, I'm not trying to push you, but it's been almost two weeks. I'm not asking that you to take on anything major, but at least let Computer run you through the Red Priorities."

"Computer will let me know if there's anything vital."

"Isn't that what 'Red Priority' means?"

Matthew remained under the hood.

"Not this week, it doesn't."

Jennifer folded her arms and looked sympathetically at her father, half his body under the hood. When she spoke again, there was a quiet desperation in her voice.

"I'm sorry, but I'm not going to let you just walk away. The Business is too important. Like it or not, you have a responsibility that you can't ignore."

Matthew finally came out from under the hood. He picked up a red rag and began cleaning the open-end wrench that he brought out with him.

"I'm not walking away from anything. I know how important the Business is. I did start it, after all. The work isn't stopping just because I spend a few days taking care of some things I've been neglecting.

"Is that what you're doing?" she asked, flatly.

Matthew looked coolly at his daughter, spoke now in a lecturing tone.

"Computer continues its daily scan of every newspaper to hit a computer system or news item to hit the wires. It continues its twenty-four hour a day monitoring of three hundred forty-three television stations and six hundred twelve radio stations."

"I know that," Jennifer stated precisely.

Matthew put down the wrench and picked up another, continued cleaning his tools.

"As we speak," he went on, "it is monitoring security systems of key locations throughout the United States and select International locations. It's monitoring Internet sites and Internet communications. It is monitoring the telecommunications activity of one thousand two hundred and four key people throughout the world. It is also tracking stock markets, financial markets, monetary values and agricultural markets, as well as numerous financial institutions."

He paused, put on a sardonic smile.

"And it is managing our portfolio. I do believe we are quite well off."

"I lack for very little," Jennifer said in a low grumble.

Matthew put down the second wrench, began methodically cleaning sockets.

"Computer continually bounces all that data around; storing, rearranging, collating, filing, processing, recalculating… and when two or more items come together just right, Computer puts it on the list. When I'm ready, Computer shows me that list. Now… when it's important enough, Computer hits me over the head with it, whether I'm ready or not."

"You have Red Priority items," said Jennifer, determined. "That makes them important."

"They'll keep." Matthew began putting his clean tools into the tall, red tool chest beside him. He indicated the nearby Bronco. "Right now, I need to realign the Bronco."

"I'll do it."

"I like doing it."

"So do I," said Jennifer.

Jennifer pulled the Bronco into one of the service bays. She climbed out of the vehicle and began hooking up the alignment equipment to the front, left tire.

She stood when she heard the sound of the Comet starting, watched as it backed out of the stall and headed for the tunnel.

The tunnel was several hundred feet long, wide enough and tall enough for a small bus and not much more. Security cameras were mounted at several locations along the way. A sensor along the route activated and a red light turned off, the green light turned on. The access door opened.

The Comet passed through, started out onto an isolated dirt

road, grassy foothills and scattered oak trees and brush. The metal access door glided smoothly and quietly closed behind it.

Back in the garage, Jennifer knelt and began making adjustments to the alignment apparatus.

"Computer, where is Dad going?" she asked.

"Indications suggest Rydel Ridge." Computer directed his voice to the nearest speaker. "Would you like me to ask him?"

Jennifer continued preparing the alignment equipment.

"No," she grumbled.

Rydel Ridge was a lookout point with a small picnic area and parking lot. It was surrounded on several sides by a grove of trees.

Downslope below the ridge was a meadow frequented by deer.

Matthew was sitting on the hood of the parked Comet. His was the only car. He was alone.

The silence was interrupted by the sound of another vehicle approaching. A small car came into the lot and pulled up near Matthew.

A teenager climbed out.

"Excuse me," he said. "Did you order the pizza?"

Matthew slid off the hood.

"You're new," he said warily.

"Sir?"

"Never mind."

The delivery person walked around to the passenger side of his car and pulled a pizza box out of a red warmer sleeve. He also came up with a small cardboard box.

"Medium combination, potato salad, and a liter of root beer."

"Did you remember the ice and a cup?" asked Matthew.

"Right here, sir," indicating the cardboard box. "Also, napkins and a fork."

Matthew took the pizza box and set it on the hood. The delivery person set the cardboard box down beside it and pulled a receipt out of his pocket.

"Your receipt," handing it to Matthew.

Matthew dropped it into the box, then handed the teenager a ten dollar bill.

"Everything looks to be here," he said.

"Aim to please." The teenager shoved the bill into his pocket and hurried back to his car.

Matthew watched him until the car was out of sight, then climbed back onto the hood. He slid the pizza box to one side of him, the cardboard box to the other.

He brought out the container of potato salad, dug around for the fork. He sat back then and continued to enjoy the day.

Finished with the alignment, Jennifer returned to the Apartment and cleaned up, then sat at the computer station. She brought up the vehicle maintenance log, began entering information on the work she'd done.

"Computer?" she prompted as she worked.

"Yes, Jennifer?"

"Sorry to bother you again..."

"Jennifer, you know very well that I am capable of carrying on conversations and responding to your requests and queries while simultaneously performing my other duties."

"Yeah, yeah, yeah… is Dad still at the Ridge?"

"The sensor indicates that Matthew is not in the vehicle. Once he left the immediate area surrounding Sutherland House, visual surveillance was discontinued. Monitoring indicates, however, that a delivery of pizza, potato salad and Mug root beer was made to Robert Matthews at the Rydel Ridge picnic grounds approximately twenty-three minutes ago. Robert Matthews is one of Matthew's current aliases."

Jennifer continued typing while half-listening to Computer.

"Sounds like his diet," she said.

"Would you like me to attempt to establish visual surveillance of the Rydel Ridge area?"

"No." Jennifer leaned back in her chair. "Let him know that I'm watching him."

There was a long pause as Computer relayed her message through the communications system in the Comet, then waited for a reply.

"Your father conveys his deep appreciation for your concern regarding his wellbeing."

Jennifer snickered at this, gave the maintenance log a final onceover before closing it, then stood and pulled a wireless keyboard from a shelf. She activated it as she started toward the couch.

"Transfer to main display, please," she said. "Bring up my game project."

The main wall display lit up as she reached the couch, her application development screen filling the display. She plopped her body down and set the keyboard in her lap.

"I am pleased to see you working on your game again, Jennifer."

Jennifer looked at one and then another of the windows on the display, each filled with C code. She moved one to the side, then another, expanded a third.

"Not much chance at school," she said. "And here... well, lately... you know."

Chapter Four

Dianna Broderick came down the stairs to the front foyer of the fine home. She looked to be in her forties. She was trim and well-maintained, wore a well-tailored dress, and had the look and air of a woman born to the life of refinement.

Two young children stood in the foyer beside their nanny. Robby was six, Thomas five.

Dianna bent down and gave each child a gentle hug. She straightened then, gave a nod to the nanny.

"Mrs. Evans," she stated flatly.

"Good morning, Mrs. Broderick," said Mrs. Evans.

"Mr. Broderick is waiting for them in his office."

"Yes, ma'am. I'll take them up."

Victor Broderick stood in front of his desk, his eye on the door. He was a tall, distinguished gentleman, looked to be in his fifties, with all the air of a high-placed, well-bred individual, fully accustomed to being in control and in charge.

Just now he was nervous.

The door opened and Mrs. Evans ushered in the two young children. They stood quietly before Victor.

"And whom do we have here, Mrs. Evans?" he asked.

Mrs. Evans placed a hand on one shoulder of each child.

"Robby, Thomas… say hello to your father."

Robby spoke in a calm, polite tone. "Hello, Father."

Thomas looked up at Victor but said nothing.

"Hello, boys," said Victor. "I've missed you."

There was an awkward silence. Victor finally clasped his hands behind his back and looked calmly down at his children. With only the slightest indication from him, Mrs. Evans moved into action.

"Off we go now, boys," she said. "You'll see your father at dinner."

Victor watched the nanny shuffle them through the door and out of sight. He stared at the open doorway.

There was absolute silence.

With a twitch of two fingers of his left hand, the door closed with a soft thump.

He stood alone in the quiet room.

§

Matthew was alone in the Apartment. The lights were dim.

He walked to the couch but remained standing.

"Computer. Activate main screen."

The wall screen lit up, though there was no data. Matthew didn't move. He stared at the wall, now faintly aglow.

"Computer…" The word drifted away into silence.

Computer waited.

"Computer…" said Matthew. Again he hesitated. Finally then, "What say we review the Red Priorities?"

"Yes, Matthew."

The picture of a young woman appeared on the display.

"The first item is the murder of Marli Reynolds."

A series of police crime scene photographs then displayed one photograph at a time.

Matthew sat down as Computer continued to review.

"Age seventeen, her body found along the bank of the Sacramento River. She was murdered elsewhere, her unclothed body dumped at the discovery site."

"Reynolds?" asked Matthew. "Doesn't ring any bells."

"Miss Reynolds' cousin, Karen Lawrence, with whom she had a close relationship, is married to Mark Gryphen."

"Son of Phillip Gryphen," stated Matthew.

"That is correct."

The photo displayed on the wall was of Marli Reynolds' naked, bruised and broken body twisted among smooth, rounded river rocks.

Matthew calmly studied the photograph.

"How was she murdered?"

A new photo displayed on the screen, this one showing Marli Reynolds on an autopsy table.

"Reports state that there was minimal bruising on the neck, yet severe internal damage."

A series of newspaper articles displayed.

"That fact was not made public," Computer continued. "There was mention of the murder on each of the local television news programs immediately following the discovery of the body, with an accompanying statement that cause of death was yet to be determined. Similar news stories were broadcast on the local radio stations."

"Just another murdered kid," said Matthew.

"Three regional newspapers carried the story, two of which had follow-ups several days later. Once again, however, the circumstances of the death were never revealed."

"The current status of the case?"

Marli Reynolds' high school picture displayed.

"Open," said Computer. "No activity. One detective assigned, and she is also working on several other cases."

Matthew stood, walked toward the picture of Marli.

"Give me the autopsy report," he said.

The first page of the report displayed. It wasn't the image of a hardcopy, but rather a computer template populated with data. Matthew read, his face shimmering against the glow of the display.

"The authorities didn't get all this, did they?"

"No."

The display changed, showed a printed hardcopy of the report. A few moments later, the hardcopy and the computer template displayed side by side.

Matthew took a moment to compare them.

"If the M.E. was trying to hide something, why bother entering one set of data into the computer and then send out a hardcopy with a different set of data?" He turned away from the display. "Have you checked to see if the data on file has changed since you first acquired this information?"

"The data on file has not changed," said Computer. "It is not consistent with the data received by the authorities."

"The difference between the two?"

"The hardcopy report contains no mention of the severity and peculiarities of the neck injuries. While the computer data identifies these injuries as the cause of death, the hardcopy report lists the cause of death simply as strangulation."

Matthew returned to the couch and sat down.

"I didn't see possible method," he said.

"None was specified."

"So, we have Marli Reynolds; tenuous connection to one of the Families. Said young lady is found murdered. Her body is obviously meant to be discovered, and in front page, albeit brief, fashion. Cause of death is unusual, and said cause is hidden from not only the public but also from the authorities."

He quickly corrected himself...

"Although the true report may have reached the authorities and was subsequently switched."

"A plausible supposition," said Computer. "Given the current facts."

"A rather violent way to get rid of a problem, isn't it? The Gryphens are nothing if not subtle."

"They may have been hoping a connection would be made to several similar murders that had been committed in previous weeks," said Computer. "A possible connection was investigated and ruled out."

"Or perhaps someone in the family did a little independent activity," said Matthew.

"Members of the Gryphen Family are not known for independent activity."

"Oh, you can bet Phillip Gryphen is seriously peeved." Matthew grew thoughtful, then came to a decision. "Continue this one on your own, Computer. You're probably right about a Society tie-in, and I would certainly like to take a crack at the Gryphens, but—"

"I will keep you informed," stated Computer.

"Next item."

The display now showed a photograph of a middle-aged man. The picture could easily be a driver's license photograph.

"Cult leader John Cutler," said Computer. "Government sources have identified his true name as Jon Willeby."

The display changed, showing John Cutler speaking before a crowd.

Computer continued.

"There have been numerous reports of Cutler performing miracles."

"That certainly wouldn't draw your attention, and most definitely not flag it as a Red Priority. I therefore assume there is a lot more going on here than simply a miracle worker at work."

"Of course," said Computer.

"Oh… I sense annoyance."

"On the contrary. I am nothing if not content… and patient."

"Okay…" Matthew said slowly. "Go on."

The reflection from the display showed on Matthew. The pale

shadows on his face shifted as the display changed.

Mary's dormitory quarters, the Academy; the rays of the setting sun were streaking in through the window, brushing across her face as she sat in her chair.

There was a sense of timeless calm in the room.

That calmness shown on Mary's face.

The Academy Headmaster eased into the chair behind his desk. He had a kind look about him. In his fifties, he had begun to gray about the edges and had a bit of late middle-aged spread.

The same sunset colors shone through the small window of his office.

There was a light on in the outer office that shone through the frosted glass pane set into the only door. The word "Headmaster" was stenciled on the glass, reverse image as seen from this side of the door,

As the Headmaster sat, the glow of the computer monitor before him reflected on his face. He stared at the words that he had written.

He spoke then, and his words appeared on the screen.

"Mary is progressing faster than we anticipated; faster than we dared hope. I sometimes sense that she is actually holding back so that we can keep up with her. As you will see in this week's enclosed report, she continues to show tremendous advancement in all six Abilities. As you well know, such is almost unprecedented. While ten percent of Society members do in fact possess talent in all six Abilities, very few of that ten percent have evidenced such latent power in all of them—and I have never witnessed such potential."

There was a long, ominous pause.

"Sir, I believe…" he paused again, began again. "I believe that Mary is much greater than we originally assessed."

The Headmaster grew silent, stared uneasily at the words on the screen.

Chapter Five

Matthew walked around the couch with a can of iced tea in hand. He climbed onto the couch and sat on the back, always with an eye to the main display on the wall. Spreadsheet text was displayed in a data window on the display; data on the third Red Priority item that Computer had presented.

Or was it the fourth…

Matthew opened his tea and took a long drink.

"All right, let's go on to the next one," he said. "This one bores me."

The displayed cleared.

"I will continue monitoring this item and keep you apprised of any developments," said Computer.

"You do that," said Matthew. "Next."

A photocopy of a newspaper article appeared on the display wall.

"The community of Andover, located in Washington State."

Matthew slid down on the couch, took another swallow.

"Make it interesting."

"Andover has a population of just over two thousand," said Computer. "It has its own hospital, doctor, dentist, water district, K-8 school, retirement center, police force, volunteer fire and emergency station, as well as a handful of stores and restaurants. There is also a lumber mill, a dairy, and several farms."

"Nice setup," said Matthew. "Nothing sinister, though. There must be hundreds of little empires just like it."

"Many small communities manage to establish some level of self-sufficiency. Few, however, have realized the level of independence as has Andover."

Photographs displayed in sequence, showing a small town nestled in the woods. These were followed by several official documents that looked to be permits, ownership certificates and business licenses.

"Can you tell me what drew you to some three-inch fluff story that a bored cub reporter dug up at county records?" asked Matthew. "And just how it has anything to do with us?"

"It is true that the item first came to my attention as a result of a small story in a weekly newspaper.

It described the turnaround and subsequent success of the town of Andover. Further investigation subsequently revealed this to be in fact a Red Priority item."

Jennifer was behind the wheel, driving the small bus down a rural, county road. There were no storefronts or homes; only an occasional lone vehicle that passed in the opposite direction.

Computer's voice disrupted the sense of solitude, coming from a speaker set in the dash.

"Jennifer?"

"Yes, Computer?"

"Your father would like to speak with you."

"Patch him through," said Jennifer.

"Jennifer." Matthew's voice sounded distant, hollow.

"Yes, Dad."

"I hear you're doing a bit of tinkering. How's the bus?"

"The rebuild on the carb did the trick," she answered.

"It just needed your magic touch," said Matthew. "Will you be coming back soon?"

"I'm about ten minutes out. Is there a problem?"

"Not at all. I think we may have an assignment."

"We?"

"If you're interested."

"I'm on my way."

Matthew and Jennifer were sitting at the table, papers scattered about on the tabletop, along with a can of iced tea and a half-full glass of water. The wall display behind them showed one of the exterior shots of the town of Andover.

"Andover was just another mill town," said Matthew. "It had a grocery store, a gas station, VFW hall, tavern, and a few hundred houses all about half a century old. But a couple of things it had going for it that most other towns of a couple of thousand people didn't have was a hospital sitting on one hill, and a school on another."

Jennifer picked up and studied a document.

"I'm guessing things started to change about… four years ago."

"About the time the mill was bought up." Matthew tapped at the document in Jennifer's hands. "It had been privately owned, but was closely allied with one of the big lumber companies. The purchase price wasn't publicly disclosed, but it was rumored, and Computer has verified, that the new owners considerably overpaid for the mill."

"Why?"

"Don't know." Matthew picked up his iced tea, took a swallow, set it back on the table. "Once they had it, they began making changes. They severed all the original ties, and lost the mill's customer base. The employees really started sweating it, especially when the mill shut down for retooling. But the new owners kept the workers on, using them to help with the renovation. They even gave raises when they reopened a few months later. The mill began bringing in its raw materials from outside the traditional markets, and began acquiring customers from the Midwest.

"So the new owners brought their suppliers and their customers with them."

"Seems that way."

"Society?"

"The connection isn't as strong as it might be, but Computer leans to yes."

"Why?"

"Not there yet," sighed Matthew. "But here are some interesting tidbits. At about the same time the mill was changing hands, the town council began changing hands as well. An overworked group of six community leaders paid a token salary of one dollar a month each. Nonetheless, they wielded what power there was in town. The town mayor had held leadership of the council for twenty-two years and showed no signs of ever letting go. Then, in a sudden and surprising turn of events, he and two others of the council were voted out, replaced by relative newcomers."

"And these have been identified as Society."

"Not yet, but…" Matthew spoke then over his shoulder. "Computer, time for some pictures."

"Please be more specific, Matthew."

"Let's start with the Addisons and go on from there."

A moment later the display showed a photograph of Robert Addison. The photograph moved to one side, allowing room for Linda Addison. Both looked to be in their thirties.

"Robert and Linda Addison," Computer stated.

Matthew turned to Jennifer.

"The Addisons showed up in Andover about four years ago."

"The same time as—"

"Right," said Matthew. "Robert is a freelance computer expert, occasionally consults to big business, writes tech books. Linda is a teacher, and it is this that is supposed to have brought them to Andover. There was an opening at the school."

The display changed. A photograph of an older man appeared. This photograph moved to one side, allowed room for a photograph of a woman. Both appeared to be in their sixties.

"Daniel and Emma Chandler," said Computer.

"Both retired," said Matthew. "Showed up in Andover a week after the Addisons. Daniel Chandler was a city planner, and Emma had been an administrator for a retirement community.

"Sounds ominous," said Jennifer, a mocking tone.

"It's all very innocent. A rundown mill gets a lift, a town council gets some new blood, a few new folks move in, breathe life into a stagnant community." Matthew stared at his can of iced tea. He took another drink. "But there's more going on. The revitalization of Andover has been carefully orchestrated. The people coming into town aren't random. Their talents mesh just a little too perfectly with the needs of the town, always at just the right time."

"Interesting," said Jennifer. "And?"

"And… Remember that I said there's been a slow influx of new people over the years. Most small towns get the occasional newcomer, but Computer has identified a point in time, beginning about six years ago, when Andover began a steady, consistent migration of new people."

"Preparing the way?"

"Which means the work actually began six years ago, not four. But the more interesting part of this is that the actual population has remained about the same."

"Oh. Very sci-fi," said Jennifer. "The town's being replaced."

"Uh-huh."

"You brought up the Addisons and the Chandlers. They've been identified as Society?"

"Still working on it," said Matthew. "I brought them up in particular because they seem to be at the center of a lot of what is going on there; as mundane and ordinary as that activity appears to be. Computer has their new names and backgrounds, their photographs, and the dates they showed up. The names and backgrounds are forged, the faces may or may not have been altered, but there are paper trails starting the day they entered Andover. Computer is working on that."

Computer displayed another picture on the wall. It was of a middle-aged man, nondescript, with no supporting text.

"Walter Carlson," said Computer.

Matthew glanced up at the image.

"Carlson, the mayor of Andover," he said. He hesitated then, looked away.

"Dad?" asked Jennifer.

Matthew's thoughts were taking him down an uncomfortable path. He looked down at his iced tea, pushed the can aside with two fingers.

"What is Victor up to?" he asked, as much to himself as to Jennifer.

Victor stood at the second floor window of his home office. Looking through the glass, he watched the two children, Robby and Thomas, in the playground that took up the left side of the backyard. The yard contained a Jungle Jim, swing set, clubhouse, and assorted bar and climbing apparatus.

The children were playing on the bars as Mrs. Evans sat on a nearby bench reading a book.

Thomas suddenly fell from the bars. Mrs. Evans was up in an instant, but almost immediately sensed that the child was unhurt. She calmly sat back down and returned to her reading.

Robby hurried to help his little brother.

Victor turned from the window. He noted a message box flashing on his computer monitor. He returned to his desk, pushed aside the chair and stood before the monitor. He clicked a key on his keyboard. The message box disappeared. He looked over at the speaker phone.

He activated the phone with a thought. A light began blinking and the sound of the dial tone could be heard.

"Get me Carlson," said Victor.

The sound of the dial tone was replaced with the sound of numeric tones as the phone dialed.

There were two rings and the phone picked up.

"Yes?" came over the phone.

"Mayor Carlson," Victor said, harshly. "What the hell is going on in Andover?"

"Mr. Broderick—" Carlson started.

"There continue to be inquiries into our activities," said Victor. "I need your assurance that all is being done that can be done to guarantee our anonymity in Andover."

"All is being done that can be done, sir."

Victor walked back to the window, looked out at his children.

He spoke over his shoulder in the general direction of the phone.

"The Andover community presents the greatest threat of exposure that we have ever faced. The peril is not only of our detection, but of our destruction."

"From Andover will come our greatest power," said Carlson through the phone's speakers.

"It is not power that we seek from Andover. It is the survival of the Society." Victor turned from the window and returned to his desk. "I've been looking over the latest reports. The conclusions from the most recent research are not as encouraging as I would hope."

"The arrival and integration of several families of... *minimal*... Abilities. This distorted the results of some of our experiments. You may also have noted the misguided directions of several Members in regards to the research. I have talked with them."

Victor responded with forced patience: "I encourage exploration, Mayor. And understand this—every member of the Society holds equal value. No one's Abilities diminish our strength—we are made stronger."

"Yes, sir," the mayor said hesitantly.

"Your reports will reflect factual data, not pretentious snobbery," Victor said sharply. "Phone off."

The light on the phone went off. Victor walked around his desk. He held out a hand and his coat came floating to him from across the room in a rush. He grasped it.

The door opened as he approached it.

Walking the second floor mezzanine, he "spoke" in *thought talk* to his wife, his words reaching out to her mind-to-mind.

"Dianna, I am more than ready for lunch. How about you?"

His wife's voice came to his mind as he reached the stairs.

"I'll be ready before you get downstairs," she said.

"On my way."

Chapter Six

Jennifer was sitting on the couch in the Apartment, reviewing the data on Victor Broderick with Computer. She was not unfamiliar with the information, but had not been around it much over the last few years.

There was a photograph of Victor on the display wall. Beside the photograph was a data window filled with text describing his Family.

Computer was providing details.

"Victor Broderick. Born 1878, Boston Massachusetts. Current residence, Boulder Colorado. He is the third Father of the Society, taking the position twenty-eight years ago upon the death of Albert Broderick, who was in turn the protégé of Jonas Westerman, the First Father and one of the three brothers who founded the Society three hundred and sixteen years ago."

The photograph on the display wall changed to one of Dianna Broderick.

"Dianna Broderick is Victor Broderick's second wife," Computer continued. "They have been married twelve years. Victor has three grown children from his first marriage and two young children from this, his second. All are Society, with his two youngest children only recently showing signs and subsequently gaining membership."

The display changed again, now showed two photographs: one of Robby and one of Thomas.

"There had been some concern," said Computer, "as both Robby and Thomas were late in showing sign."

"What are their Abilities?" asked Jennifer.

"I have yet to access information regarding the nature of their Abilities."

"Victor has four," recalled Jennifer. "How many does Dianna have?"

"Dianna Broderick has two— thought talk and telekinesis, both at high levels."

Jennifer nodded slowly, her mind drifting. Possessing two of the six Abilities was fairly common among Society members. Victor having four was rare; possessing four at high levels was very rare.

"Victor's grown children… if I remember right, they're not that much older than I am."

Three photographs appeared on the display, one at a time, each making way for the next until they were all showing side by side.

"Vincent, Carl and Anna," said Computer. "All are in their thirties."

"Which means Victor waited quite a while before having children."

The displayed changed again, this time to a candid photograph of Victor and an unidentified woman walking on a beach. By their apparel and the look of the photograph, the era was dated to nineteen twenties.

"By traditional standards, yes," said Computer. "However, many Society members choose to wait. As you may recall, Jennifer, no

Society member can live under the same roof with an outsider, not even if that outsider is the Member's child. Until that child shows sign and also becomes a member, it must live elsewhere, and remain unaware of the existence of the Society."

"Or… the family can be Grey Caste," said Jennifer.

Matthew climbed off the access ladder and entered the Apartment as Computer and Jennifer continued their conversation. He quietly went into the kitchen.

"That is true," said Computer. "A special status was created approximately twenty years ago that allow Society members to live with non-Society, but only under special circumstances and under very severe restrictions. Such level of Society membership is known as Grey Caste."

"How many Grey Caste are there?" asked Jennifer.

"I do not have the most current information," said Computer. "I will begin the research and attempt to extrapolate an approximate number for you. I am afraid there is a high probability that I will not be able to acquire an exact figure."

"Don't sweat it. Cancel that research; it isn't important."

Matthew came up behind the couch, a can of iced tea in hand.

"Society population, twelve thousand, of which fewer than two hundred are Grey Caste at any one time," he said matter-of-factly. He opened his can of iced tea with a loud pop.

"Geez, Dad." Jennifer jumped, startled. "Where'd you come from?"

Matthew climbed up onto the back of the couch and sat with his feet on the cushions.

"History lesson?"

"All morning. I thought it was time for a review." She settled back. "You hang out with a scary bunch of folks."

"You can't choose your family."

There was an awkward pause, after which Matthew slid down and sat beside Jennifer. She laid her head back.

"Even growing up with this, it all seems way too bizarre. I can study the story of the Society from its very beginnings, and I can make myself believe that it all makes sense. But when I climb up that ladder and go back into the real world, none of it makes sense. None of it seems right. None of it… belongs. We don't belong; up there or down here."

The display showed another photograph of Victor.

"Like it or not, we were born of the Society," said Matthew. "Whether Victor Broderick likes it or not."

"Not," Jennifer stated.

"The Sutherland family was, and is, one of the seventeen Primary Families of the Society." Matthew fell into a calm melancholy. "Whether we like it or not, you and I have to somehow live in both worlds."

After a moment of appropriate silence, Computer spoke up.

"Eleven thousand, three hundred and fifty five."

Matthew glanced up. "What?"

"Society population is eleven thousand, three hundred and fifty five, of which three thousand, two hundred are of the Primary families, the remainder are of the Lesser Families."

"Have you been sulking?" asked Matthew.

"I do not sulk. Your figure of twelve thousand was imprecise."

"I do worry about you."

"There is no need," said Computer. "I continually monitor the status of all my components and perform scheduled diagnostics. Any deviations are corrected and any requiring human interactions are always reported to you in a timely manner."

"Now you're being deliberately obtuse," said Matthew.

Chapter Seven

Victor helped Robby and Thomas out of the large sedan while looking with satisfaction at the grounds and stately buildings of the Academy. They walked from the car and onto the grounds proper, followed the walkway that would take them beneath the great oak tree in the center of the grounds.

"The Academy is a wonderful old institution," Victor said to his children. "While you have attained Society membership, all members must complete their instruction here prior to attaining full rights."

He indicated a new building off to their right.

"That building over there is the dormitory," he said. "For many, it is easier to stay here on the campus while attending. You of course will be coming home to your mother and me each afternoon."

They passed beneath the tree. Victor saw Mary sitting high up in the branches. He spoke to her using thought talk, mind to mind.

"Good morning, Mary."

There was no immediate response. However, as they continued on toward the Academy main building, her words brushed his mind:

"Good morning."

Victor and his children continued to the administration building, climbed the steps and entered the foyer.

The security guard, a large, broad-shouldered man, was sitting behind a desk. He watched the new arrivals approach.

"Good morning, Father," he said. "The Headmaster is expecting you."

"Thank you, Jim," said Victor.

Victor led his children down the hall. They passed through the outer vestibule and into the Headmaster's office. The Headmaster stood behind his desk, gave a deep nod and waved a hand for Victor and his children to be seated.

"Good morning, Father," said the Headmaster.

"Good morning, Headmaster." Victor sat down, watched his children take their seats. He turned again to the Headmaster. "I saw Mary outside."

"In the tree again?" Headmaster said aloud, continued then in thought talk, mind to mind. "You saw my report?"

"I agree with your assessment," Victor answered in thought talk.

He looked to his children, again to Headmaster, spoke aloud.

"You remember Robby and Thomas?" he asked. "They are very excited about getting started."

"We've talked many times." Headmaster smiled at the children. "So, you are looking forward to beginning your classes, then?"

The children gave obligatory nods and Headmaster turned his attention back to Victor.

"They will do very well here, Father. They are quite bright and very talented."

Headmaster placed his forearms on his desk and his expression grew fixed. He and Victor spoke now in thought talk.

"You've read the details on Mary's signs?"

"I am quite pleased by the reports," Victor sent back.

"You are not concerned?"

"Concerned? Not at all. She may well be everything we hoped for."

"And then some."

"All the better."

"I of course bow to your judgment, Father."

The boys looked first to Victor, then to Headmaster, then back again. They knew there was a conversation going on that they weren't witness to.

Victor looked side-glance at them. He gave them a wink, then spoke aloud to Headmaster.

"Continue to voice your concerns, Headmaster. And by all means, proceed with due caution.

Do not, however, attempt to inhibit her growth in any way."

He looked again to the children, smiled broadly.

"I am quite proud of my children. I have no doubts regarding their success at the Academy."

"You may leave them in my care, Father."

"Yes. Yes, of course." Victor showed no indications of leaving.

Headmaster smiled patiently.

"They will be waiting for you when you return for them this afternoon," he said.

"Yes."

It took another few moments for Victor to stand. Headmaster stood then, his expression sympathetic.

"No easier the second time around, is it?" he asked.

"Was I as anxious with the other children?"

"I had quite the time getting you to leave," said the Headmaster.

"Well... I'll not cause a scene this time around." He knelt before the children and spoke warmly to them. "I'll be back this afternoon. And don't forget... the most important thing is to enjoy yourselves. You pay attention to what you are told, and do your best; but do not forget to have fun."

He stood again and looked back to the Headmaster.

"Until this afternoon."

Headmaster watched Victor leave the room, then smiled comfortingly at the children, sitting patiently in their chairs. He sensed both anxiety and anticipation from them.

Good.

§

Victor came out onto the front steps of the Academy main building. He stopped to admire the view and take in the moment. The sun was shining, the air was fresh and clear. He heard the sound of children laughing somewhere in the distance.

He looked over at the large tree in which he had seen Mary, then took the steps and starting along the walk toward the tree.

He reached out to Mary in thought talk while still some distance from the tree.

"Mary?"

There was no response. As he came nearer, he could see that she was still in the branches.

"Good morning to you again, Mary," he sent to her.

He was within a few steps of the tree.

"Good morning, Father," she sent to him, mind-to-mind.

Victor passed under the tree, continued walking.

"And how are you doing?" he asked her. "Are you enjoying your time here?"

"I have no complaints."

"I am very glad to hear that." Victor was getting near his car. "Shouldn't you be in class?"

"I am in class."

"I see," said Victor. "I do like your classroom. But I recall that mornings are usually devoted to more traditional activity; reading, writing, arithmetic."

"I am special."

Victor smiled to himself, though he suspected she could sense that. He reached his car. There was a moment of silence.

"Father… would you like me to keep an eye on your children?"

"Thank you, Mary. I would be honored."

There was a pallet of bricks sitting on the walkway. Matthew was on his knees in front of a partially completed retaining wall that bordered the walk and enclosed a raised flowerbed.

It was another nice day, but there were clouds on the horizon.

Sam came up with a wheelbarrow load of prepared mortar mix. Matthew looked in the wheelbarrow, pushed a trowel into the mixture.

"It looks good, Sam."

"You really ought to get a mixer," said Sam.

Matthew gave Sam a devilish grin, turned back to his work without responding.

"Yeah, yeah… I know," Sam sighed. "You already have one."

"It's good for you," said Matthew.

Jennifer came down the walkway from the direction of the front of the house. Sam turned his attention to her. Seeing Sam's distraction, Matthew turned his head enough to see his daughter coming.

He gave a knowing glance to Sam, returned to his work.

Jennifer looked vaguely perturbed at Sam's presence.

"Hello, Sam."

"Hi, Jen." Sam indicated their work. "What do you think?"

"Not bad." She looked to her father then. "Are you going to run it all the way down the walk?"

"I'll enclose this bed." He used the trowel to point to the other side of the walkway. "Can't make up my mind about the other side, though."

Sam spoke up: "I told him he should do the same to both sides of the walk."

Jennifer studied the walkway, trying to give her father's dilemma the attention it deserved.

"Yeah, well, you know my dad," she said. "Once he's built, planted or grown something, why do it again?" She indicated the grounds all about them. "These grounds are testimony to his 'now let's try it this way' philosophy."

"I like it here," said Sam.

"I know." Jennifer folded her arms across her chest, turned her attention back to her father. "How much longer are you going to be, Dad?"

Matthew didn't miss a beat, continued working.

"Something up?" he asked.

"Nothing that can't wait a few minutes." She glanced up, away, to the house. "Some info has come in on one of the projects we've been working on."

"Right. Let me get through this last batch of mortar. I'll be in once we get things cleaned up."

Sam took a look at the approaching clouds. They looked dark.

"We should cover this wall in plastic, Mr. Sutherland. It looks like it might rain later."

"Good man, Sam," said Matthew. "See what you can find in the shed."

Sam hesitated. He knew that Jennifer would be gone when he got back.

She made it easy for him by turning and returning to the front of the house. At that, Sam headed to the shed in the yard at the back of the house.

Matthew looked to his left and then his right at the receding figures of Sam and Jennifer. He allowed himself a chuckle, as if he had somehow done something.

Chapter Eight

Matthew stepped off the ladder, walked across the Apartment and stood beside Jennifer, before the wall display.

"Computer has more info on Andover," said Jennifer.

"Give it to me, Computer," said Matthew.

"Please specify, Matthew."

Matthew rubbed his forehead, his temple.

"You know what I'm asking, Computer. It's not like you weren't listening."

There was a long, awkward silence. Matthew waited for Computer to begin the review, Jennifer watched Matthew grow more impatient, and Computer stubbornly waited for Matthew to be more specific.

Matthew finally surrendered.

"Computer. Jennifer tells me that you have more information regarding the Andover situation. When you have a moment, will you fill us in?"

"It is one of my functions, Matthew."

"It certainly is."

The display wall before them lit up with a photograph of Carlson, the mayor of Andover. The picture moved to one side, making room for a data window of text.

The display lasted for several seconds, after which the photo and text disappeared, to be replaced with a photograph of Robert Addison, which slid to one side, making room for its data window of text.

Computer spoke as these and then additional displays came and went.

"The fabricated pasts of the Society members in Andover are quite thorough. There are completed life histories for each of them."

"I'm sure that didn't slow you down much," said Matthew. "You've ID'd them?"

"All have been identified."

"Good work."

"Thank you, Matthew," said Computer. "Each new arrival in Andover coincided with the disappearance of a Society member elsewhere, sometimes to within several weeks."

"Then it should have been fairly easy for you, shouldn't it?"

"Once my research made a connection between the disappearance in one location and an appearance in Andover, it was not difficult to make a positive match."

Matthew looked side glance to Jennifer.

"Computer keeps track of as many Members as he can, but it's impossible to always know where every individual is at any given moment. When one drops out of sight and doesn't surface again…" he leaned near his daughter and whispered, "… it drives him a little batty."

Matthew was sitting on the couch, looking up at the wall display. It was showing a photograph of the street intersection in Andover that made up the downtown.

Jennifer was standing behind the couch, leaning back against it, facing away from the display.

"It will be just a quick trip," said Matthew.

"To do what?" asked Jennifer. She folded her arms, stared down at her feet. "We still don't have any idea what it's all about."

"Exactly."

Jennifer shook her head, pushed off the couch, turned around and climbed onto the back of the couch.

"Then what good will it do? Dad, we need to get more info before we start poking our noses around up there."

"I gotta see what the fuss is about."

"Then I'll go with you."

"It's a simple recon." Matthew shifted on the couch to face Jennifer. "I'll be in and out of there in a day. Better if you're here to keep Computer from getting lazy. You said yourself—we need more info. You stay here and keep digging."

"Am I in the Family Business or not?"

"Up to your armpits. Don't you worry. There will be ample opportunity for you to risk your neck. First Recon is a one-person job. This time out, that's me."

Jennifer frowned, slid down from the back of the couch to the seat.

"Yeah, well, I don't like it."

"Neither did your mother."

Chapter Nine

Matthew guided his pickup alongside the pumps at the Andover Quickstop, stopped and turned off the engine. He climbed out and moved to the pump. He took in the community as he filled the tank.

The downtown area consisted of a handful of retail storefronts and a long building housing the town hall, police station, mayor's office and volunteer fire house.

The scene was a strange mix of the normal and the surreal, everyday sights and sounds filtered through an ethereal haze.

A police car pulled up along the other side of the pumps and the police chief climbed out and began pumping gas. He glanced warily at Matthew. There was a visible air of barely suppressed enmity in the way he looked at this stranger to his town.

The gas nozzle clicked off. Matthew returned it to the pump, put the gas cap back on, and walked to the open door of the store.

A young woman stood behind the counter near the register. Matthew got in line behind two men and a woman. The two men stepped up to the counter together.

"Hey, Meg," said one. "Give me the chicken and Jo-Jos."

"Me too," said the other. They were on a lunch break from the mill.

"You got it." Meg moved to one side to put together the baskets.

The first man leaned a hip against the counter and frowned.

"Man, I don't wanna go back in there today."

"What do you got to whine about, Carl?" said the second. "All you do is sit up there and bitch all day. You don't do a damn thing."

"Yeah? Like you got it so tough."

"I'm not the one doin' the whining."

"Yeah?" Carl tried to hide a grin. "How 'bout I kick your ass? We'll see some whining, then."

"Don't tire yourself."

Meg brought the two baskets over, started to ring up the totals. Carl put a bill on the counter.

"I got 'em, Meg," he said.

"Thank you, Carl." She picked up the money, opened the register and put the bill into the slot.

The police chief came into the store, stood in line behind Matthew. There was a sudden, definite change in the air; a heavy silence, though no one outwardly acted any differently.

Carl and his buddy picked up their lunch baskets and started toward the door.

"I say we grab a coupla' beers to go with these and head in the opposite direction," said Carl.

"Sounds great," the other said doubtfully. "And do what?"

"Anything. Anything we want."

"Yeah... you gotta give me more than that."

Outside, they started across the parking lot and in the direction of the mill.

The line at the counter moved forward and the woman put her few things on the counter.

"Is this it for you, Angie?" asked Meg.

"All for today, Meg."

Meg rang up the items and began putting them into a bag.

"Nine forty," she said.

Angela handed Meg a ten dollar bill. Meg looked past Angela and Matthew to the police chief as she gave Angela her change. Angela smiled uncomfortably as she quickly gathered her things.

"Thank you," she said. She started toward the door.

Matthew moved up to the counter, pulled his wallet out and held it ready. The police chief was close behind him.

"Welcome to Andover," said Meg. She seemed distracted.

"Thank you," said Matthew. "Pump one."

"Anything else?"

"Just the gas, thanks."

"Eighteen even," said Meg, not looking at the pump register.

Matthew pulled out eighteen dollars. Handing it to Meg, he glanced back over his shoulder. The police chief stood silent, looking directly at him.

Matthew turned back to Meg.

"Where's a good place for a sit-down lunch?" he asked.

There was a long moment of heavy quiet when nothing appeared to happen.

"Sally's," Meg said at last. "Right around the corner."

"Thank you." Matthew moved away from the counter.

"Sure thing. Come again."

Matthew started away from the counter, hesitated as he reached the door. Looking back into the store, the police chief hadn't moved to the counter, was watching him. Meg, her hands resting on the counter, managed a smile in Matthew's direction.

"Thanks, Meg," said Matthew. "I'll do that."

Matthew turned the pickup into an available parking space in front of Sally's Café, a low structure with a flat roof, a wall of windows with the front door at one end of the building. He took a leisurely look around before slowly walking to the door.

The café was two-thirds full. Jan, the waitress, approached and directed Matthew to an open booth.

Robert Addison and his wife Linda were in the booth next to his. Robert watched Jan fill the stranger's water glass and take his order.

"Carlson's right," Robert said in thought talk. "It's him."

"Probably," Linda sent back, mind-to-mind.

"It's him," Robert returned. "Did you see the way he took in the room? He picked out every Member here, almost instantly. Who else could do that?"

Daniel and Emma Chandler came into the café. Robert watched as Matthew quickly took in the Chandlers, then appeared to ignore them.

"Daniel! Emma!" Jan said, coming up to them. She called back in the direction of the kitchen. "Sally! Come out here!"

Sally, a middle-aged woman dressed in black slacks and a brightly colored blouse, came out from the back to greet them. Robert divided his attention between Matthew sitting in his booth and Sally greeting the Chandlers.

"Did you see how he reacted to the Chandlers coming in?" Robert sent to his wife.

"No, I'm sorry. Not really," Linda said aloud, in a low voice.

Matthew was absently watching Sally talking with the Chandler's at their booth when Jan came with Matthew's lunch of burger, fries and iced tea. While not overly friendly, Jan was polite enough.

"Will there be anything else?" she asked.

"Not just now. Thanks."

"Enjoy your lunch, hon," she said, starting away.

Matthew took a bite of his hamburger, munched on a couple of fries. He took his time. As he ate, he listened.

In addition to the normal sounds of people at lunch, there was something else; an undercurrent of sound. There was a noise, a hissing sound of thoughts and words, all just under the surface. Matthew was able to snatch a word here and there.

He casually glanced at the Addisons in the next booth. He caught Robert glaring at him before he slowly turned away.

Matthew continued eating, observing... and listening.

§

Robert turned his head, slowly, until he was looking directly at Matthew. He reached down and took hold of Linda's hand. She looked at him, then looked around the room.

There were occasional bursts of static in the background. The subvocal whispers grew suddenly louder... then stopped.

Robert continued looking at Matthew. He watched Matthew slowly put down his hamburger and take a drink of his iced tea.

There were several sudden, flashing images of Matthew's past, pictures of Matthew Sutherland: with his daughter, with Computer, with his vehicles, with Sam; with Sharon, his wife.

Sudden, rushing close-up of Matthew's face Present Time; a barely perceptible movement of his eyes. At that instant, Robert was visibly thrown back into his seat.

Linda and several others turned quickly and looked at Robert; Robert sat stunned.

"Did you see that?" He asked aloud, a harsh whisper. "Did you feel that? He did that on his own!"

Matthew calmly finished his hamburger.

The subvocal hissing whispers continued to intensify. Matthew caught quick words of violence among the static.

He finished his French fries, took another drink from his iced tea.

He caught then, very clearly, Robert saying subvocally: "We should kill him now."

Matthew calmly took another drink from his iced tea.

Chapter Ten

Jennifer came from the back of the main house, turning off lights along the way. Coming into the foyer, she made sure the front door was locked. She glanced out the window before heading down the hall toward the door to the basement.

She worked her way down to the Apartment. The room was quiet but for the faint hum of the computer equipment.

"Any word, Computer?"

"Your father left Andover thirty five minutes ago," said Computer. "He should be checking into the hotel in Olympia within the hour."

Jennifer slid onto the couch, pulled her feet up and wrapped her arms comfortably around her legs.

"Why didn't you tell me?"

"I am not permitted to communicate with you while you are upstairs unless there is an emergency or I am specifically directed to do so. I monitor the grounds for intrusion or other danger, but am programmed to disregard all personal—"

"Stop," Jennifer cut him off. "Ya' know, I think there's a lot more going on in those vacuum tubes of yours than you let on."

"As you are well aware, Jennifer, vacuum tubes have not been used in the manufacture of compu—"

"I know that."

There was a long pause. Both were silent.

"And you know that I know that," said Jennifer. Another pause. "Computer?"

"Yes, Jennifer?"

"You always know the right thing to say."

"It is the way Matthew programmed me."

"Sure." Jennifer smiled nostalgically. "You and I have both done some growing since then."

"Yes, Jennifer," Computer stated matter-of-factly. Several moments later then: "Upon his departure from Andover, Matthew stated that all went well. He will be making a full report once he checks into his room."

"Anything else?"

"He asked how you were."

"You can tell him that I'm all alone in a hole in the ground, getting ready to eat leftovers."

"Sensors indicate that Matthew is no longer in the vehicle. I will attempt to deliver your message when—"

"Stop toying with me."

"Jennifer, I—"

"He's out of the pickup?"

"The sensor indicates that no one is in the vehicle."

"How long ago?"

"I cancelled constant monitoring of that sensor once Matthew left the Andover community, whereupon I returned to intermittent check mode," said Computer. "I sought current sensor status immediately prior to attempting to deliver your message."

"Then he must be—"

"Excuse me, Jennifer. Matthew's John Marshall credit card has just been used to register into the hotel."

Jennifer let out a sigh of relief. Computer continued.

"John Marshall is the identity selected to indicate that all is well and that there is no duress."

"I need something to eat," said Jennifer.

She stood and went to the kitchen. Opening the refrigerator, she brought out a bowl of leftovers, shook her head in bewilderment.

"If there hadn't been computers, Dad would have had to invent them," she said. "There's no way he could have played these games without you to keep track of all this crap."

Computer responded calmly and without emotion, as always.

"I keep your father alive."

Jennifer was numbed by the statement. She stood before the microwave, bowl in hand.

The silence hung heavy in the air.

"Matthew has made Internet contact," said Computer. "Report begins."

The hotel room was clean, comfortable, but nothing special. Matthew was sitting at the desk. The report finished, he turned off his laptop. He stared at the darkening display a moment, then slid the chair back and stood up.

He walked across the room, leaned a shoulder tiredly against the wall beside the draped window; he looked absently back into the room; something was brushing at his mind; something nearby... something... bad.

Outside, the night was dark, wet. Across the narrow parking lot, Robert Addison was sitting on the hood of a car. He appeared calm, his feet on the bumper, elbows on his knees and hands clasped.

Victor's home office was lit only by a single lamp. Victor was sitting at his desk, a photograph in his hand. It showed Matthew Sutherland standing in line at the counter in the Andover Quickstop.

He tossed the picture onto the desk. He rubbed his face with his hands, turned his chair until he was facing the dark window.

"Damn," he grumbled.

Dianna was standing in the doorway, little more than a silhouette.

"What does he know?" she asked.

"Enough." Victor turned about in his chair and pulled the photograph to him. He stared at it, frowning. He pushed it aside again. "His way of letting us know that he's onto us. But it was recon. He knows we're up to something, but not what or why."

"Victor…" She moved into the room.

"Damn him."

"This project is too important to let Matthew—"

"Yes, yes," Victor said irritably. He turned away from Dianna. "As Father, my first duty is to protect the Society. My second duty is to the prosperity of the members of the Society." He turned back. "By inference, my third duty is to ensure the survival of the Andover project."

"He has left you with no alternative."

"For decades, he has been little more than a thorn in my side, never really a serious threat. Lately..."

"If only—"

"Yes," said Victor. "When Sharon..."

"What else could we do?"

"I know. And now..." Victor rested his head against the back of the chair. "That damnable computer creation of his. If anything happens to him or his daughter, everything they know about the Society will be sent out to dozens of news organizations around the world."

"So, what do we do, Victor?"

"As you said, we have no choice. And the longer we delay, the more difficult it will be. It's obvious that his daughter is being groomed to join the family business." He let out a tired sigh. "How did we come to this?"

"You can't blame yourself, my love," said Dianna. "You have done everything possible to avoid what Matthew has made inevitable."

Chapter Eleven

The Andover Elementary School was little more than a handful of administration offices, a row of classrooms, and the auditorium, which also served as cafeteria and school gym.

There were eight cars in the small parking lot. To the east, the horizon was just beginning to turn a predawn pink.

A ninth car pulled into the lot. Daniel Chandler and his wife Emma got out, walked across the lot and approached the front doors.

The police chief stood in the foyer. The Chandlers said nothing as they passed him.

There were several dozen people in the auditorium, gathered in groups of three and four. Some were talking aloud, others subvocally using thought talk.

The mayor was in deep conversation with Linda Addison, Meg and Angela. Linda looked anxious, yet excited. When the mayor saw the Chandlers enter the auditorium, he waved them over to join them.

"Welcome," he said, shaking Daniel's hand.

"Good evening, Mayor," said Daniel.

"Hello, Tom," said Emma.

Daniel quickly scanned the room, looked briefly at each of those gathered. He turned again to the mayor, spoke to the entire group.

"I'm glad to see that Victor has finally decided to put an end to the Sutherland problem."

Meg and Angela bristled at the comment. The mayor, however, maintained his vague political face.

"It had to have been a difficult decision for Father to make, Dan."

"Quite," Emma agreed. "Everyone knows how close Victor and Matthew once were."

"Everyone also knows the threat that he poses to the Society," said Daniel.

Linda Addison pushed aside her anxiety.

"He shall be dealt with tonight," she said.

"We all hope so," said Daniel.

"No time for doubts, my friend," said Mayor Carlson.

"Matthew Sutherland is not a threat to be dealt with lightly."

"We were recently witness to that," agreed Emma.

Linda gave a sharp, sure nod.

"We will not be caught unawares again, Emma," she said.

Emma gave Linda a faint smile, spoke with a barely hidden patronizing tone.

"Of course not," she said.

"Robert is not totally without his own strengths," said Linda. "With mine to support him, and through me all of yours, Matthew Sutherland will not be a problem."

Meg stepped into the conversation for the first time.

"What about that AI of his?" she asked.

The mayor responded with an air of authority.

"The Father will make contact with it the moment Matthew has been dealt with. A truce will be offered—Jennifer will remain unharmed so long as the computer does not release Society information."

Daniel nodded agreement, "Victor is certain that Matthew has made his daughter's safety the computer's number one directive."

"Once the truce is made," said the mayor, "we will have all the time we need to complete the Andover project and find a way to deal with Jennifer Sutherland and the threat the Sutherland computer holds over us."

The police chief came into the auditorium then, ceremoniously closed the doors behind him. It took several moments for the room to grow quiet, during which time everyone in the room grew introspective.

Linda Addison wound her way through the people and into the middle of the room. The others in the room began to drift toward her. She calmly and unhurriedly turned about in a circle and stopped. She moved her feet apart, held her arms slightly out, palms out.

She closed her eyes...

Robert Addison slid off the hood, stood beside his car. He looked over the hood to the hotel, the outside room doors even spaced, alternating with large, draped windows. Behind him, a wall of trees bordered the parking lot.

He took a long, deep breath.

In the Andover Elementary auditorium, Linda smiled. She breathed deep, moved her arms further away from her body.

She made contact.

Eight people in the auditorium formed a circle around her. Holding their arms out, their hands just touched. As others in the auditorium began closing in around the circle, the eight laid their heads back and closed their eyes.

In the hotel parking lot, Robert Addison took in strength, swallowed energy.

An old neighborhood in Andover, just before dawn; it was wet outside.

A middle-aged woman came out onto her porch. Next door, another stepped outside, onto her porch.

Half a dozen homes, half a century old... neighbors came out onto their porches. They looked up into the predawn sky. They spread their arms, hands, palms out.

They closed their eyes...

In the auditorium, those outside the circle of eight had formed a larger outer circle.

In the parking lot, Robert Addison moved away from the car.

Matthew stood in the middle of his hotel room. The only light was that leaking in from around the sides of the drapes, sending shadows across Matthew's face and frame.

He gave a glance to his laptop, which was still sitting on the desk across the room. With the casual flick of two of his fingers, the display shattered and whorls of smoke came up through the keys.

He went to the door, opened it and stepped outside.

Arms loose at his sides, he twitched a finger. The door closed behind him.

There were seven vehicles in the lot, including his pickup. The predawn air was wet, the asphalt and cars shimmering with the damp.

Robert Addison was standing near the treeline bordering the parking lot.

Matthew took a step from the porch of his hotel room.

Suddenly then the parking lot, the hotel, the surrounding world... all spun dizzily... all went fuzzy...

The world cleared then, refocused; the hotel, the parking lot.

Robert Addison was looking down the treeline... to where Matthew now stood, some forty feet away.

They eyed each other, studied each other…

Robert twitched a hand, almost imperceptibly. The large tree beside him ripped from the soil, uprooted, and was tossed toward Matthew.

With a tilt of the head, Matthew shattered the tree in midair. A thousand large splinters rained onto the parking lot.

Five of the largest splinters lifted up from the asphalt and rushed at Matthew.

He casually lifted a hand. The wood exploded into a cloud of powder in front of him.

He tilted his head, twitched. Six medium sized trees, still standing upright, rushed toward Robert, surrounded him, closed in tightly around him.

Robert flicked two fingers. The trees exploded into thick chunks of sawdust, leaving Robert standing unharmed in the dusty cloud.

In the elementary school auditorium, Linda was standing inside the circle of eight, the larger circle beyond. Her hair was limp, her skin shiny and pasty. Her arms trembled slightly.

On the porches of the old neighborhood, men and women stood unmoving, arms out, hands out, heads back with eyes closed; faces pasty, hair hanging damp.

Robert turned his head, looked back to his car. He spun his head back then. The car lifted off the ground, turned on its side and rushed at Matthew.

Matthew looked at the car and the metal of the vehicle was crushed in midair. The car spun about and rushed back toward Robert.

Robert swung his arm and the car was flung back into the parking lot, crashing down onto its wheels.

Matthew took the moment to look sharply at Robert. Robert was pushed violently back, as if from a blow. He stumbled but remained standing.

In the auditorium, Linda's eyes opened wide and she sucked in a throaty breath.

On a porch in the old neighborhood, a middle-aged woman fell to her knees, clutched at her chest. She reached out to the porch rail, her face taut with surprise and pain.

In the auditorium, tears ran down Linda's cheek.

She was suddenly afraid.

Matthew took a step nearer Robert, then another. He ignored the trees and cars. He focused on Robert.

Robert cried out in pain. He twisted in distress. He tried to fight back, but Matthew easily tossed the attempts aside. Matthew took another step, and another, moved methodically closer to Robert. Robert shuddered at every slight twitch or flick from Matthew.

Robert fell to his knees.

Matthew took a final step, six feet from Robert. Matthew's expression was calm but determined.

Robert let out a piercing mind scream.

In the elementary school auditorium, Linda fell to her knees and let out her own mind scream. Those around her were thrown violently backward, some stumbling to remain standing, many thrown hard to the hardwood floor.

On the porches of the old neighborhood, neighbors thrown back against the wall fell to their knees, fell forward.

Matthew looked away from Robert Addison's body. He started across the parking lot. The debris that littered the lot moved out of his path as he walked to his pickup. Debris that covered his pickup was thrown clear.

He climbed in behind the wheel.

There was a clear path out of the parking lot.

§

Victor stood at the window, gray early morning light glowing dully on his face. It streamed past him and into the room, his office in heavy shadow.

He turned to his wife, standing in middle of the room. She held her arms stiffly at her sides, a look of desperation on her face that she tried to hide with a false calm reassurance.

Something bad had happened. They both sensed it, felt it.

Victor set his own expression...

He was Father.

They would overcome whatever was out there.

He turned back to the window, clasped his hands behind his back.

§

Mary was sitting in the wooden chair in the middle of her small room. She was looking in the direction of her window. The curtain was pulled aside, the gray light of early morning streaming in.

While there was a calmness in her expression, there was little emotion visible on her young face

Chapter Twelve

The lights of the Apartment were set to dim, the glow from the rows of active security monitors pushing into the middle of the room. Matthew was sitting at the kitchen counter, his back to the room, absently dunking a tea bag in a cup of hot water.

Jennifer stepped off the access ladder and into the room. She walked across the room and came up behind Matthew. She hugged her father about the shoulders, moved around beside him and climbed onto the empty stool next to him.

"Feeling any better?" she asked.

"I'm fine," said Matthew.

Jennifer nodded slowly, not completely convinced, but decided to let it go.

"Sam came by today," she said. "Looking for you."

Matthew lifted the tea bag out and set it on the saucer.

"He's a good kid," he said.

"Uh, huh."

"What time is it?" He rubbed at his tired eyes.

"About eleven thirty."

"Night?"

"Uh, huh."

"Damn." He turned and slid off the stool.

He reached back, picked up his cup of tea and carried it over to the table. He sat down and leaned back in the chair.

Jennifer followed and sat in the chair opposite. She studied him a moment.

"Well?" she finally asked.

Matthew looked up, looked across the table to his daughter. Their eyes locked and each seemed to be searching out the other. He finally leaned forward, however hesitantly, and set the cup of tea on the table.

"Everyone was watching, Jen," he said. "Everyone. Pushing. I wasn't fighting just Addison. I was fighting the whole town. They were feeding him."

"I've never heard of that," said Jennifer. "I mean, I've heard of linking, but it's always one member supporting another; never a group."

"Me either. A few with the ability to support, like Addison's wife." Matthew frowned. "This was more. She... funneled. Like a conduit. I was facing all of them; from all over Andover."

Jennifer reached out and rested a hand on her father's forearm.

"And you won."

"I don't think we won anything."

"I don't understand."

Matthew leaned back again, spoke into the air.

"Computer," he said. "Update, please."

"Andover population is eighty three percent evacuated," said Computer.

"Current location of evacuees?"

"Unknown."

Matthew turned again to Jennifer.

"They began leaving almost immediately; most likely following a pre-established emergency plan."

"So you won," Jennifer stated again. "Whatever they were planning, it's not happening."

"Delayed, maybe," he said, sighing. "And we don't know what *it* is. We have no idea what their goal was for Andover, or if this funneling had any part in it."

"We know that you have the strength to stand against a whole town."

Matthew shook his head and leaned further forward.

"Nope. That's just one more question," he said. "It shouldn't have been possible. Not even close."

Jennifer had no response to that. She knew that he was right. There was no way her father should have been able to take on an entire town, whatever the inherent strength of his Abilities.

"We can assume the few folks remaining in Andover are not Society," she said, redirecting the conversation. "They have to be confused right about now. And there are going to be a few stories hitting the wires."

"So true."

"We can also assume that Computer will be in Batty Mode for the next few weeks, looking for signs of where our Andover refugees went."

"Also true." Matthew reached out and picked up his tea. He took a sip. It was already getting cold.

He set the cup back on the table, pushed it aside.

"Let's put ourselves in Victor's shoes," said Jennifer. "We may not know the goal they've set for themselves, but we may be able to extrapolate what Victor's next step might be."

"Maybe." Matthew leaned back, fought back a yawn. "But not tonight."

Victor climbed out of his car, looked up into the sunny sky as he gently closed the door. He turned about then and started across the Academy grounds, following the winding concrete walk. He slowed as he reached the great Oak tree, stopped once he was beneath its wide branches.

He stepped up to the gnarly trunk, leaned against the bark.

He spoke aloud, without looking up into canopy.

"You were there," he said.

Mary didn't respond at first.

"I was," she said finally, also speaking aloud.

"Mary…" he started. "Why did you help him?"

"I did very little."

"It was enough."

"Yes," she said. "I had no choice."

"That isn't true," said Victor. "You had a choice. You could have stayed out of it."

Mary said nothing.

"I thought we were friends, Mary."

"The Society must come first, Father."

"Always," said Victor. "Absolutely."

"Everything that happened, had to happen."

"Your Sight is not developed, Mary," said Victor, frowning and shaking his head. "It is untrained.

Taking actions on it now is dangerous."

"I know what I know."

"And what is it that you know?" Victor asked. "Must Matthew live in order for the Society to survive?"

"No."

"Then what? We have been set back months, maybe years. Is that a good thing?"

Mary hesitated.

"What happened, had to happen," she said then, basically repeating what she had said a moment before.

Victor pushed away from the tree and started slowly away.

He spoke to her then in thought talk, mind-to-mind.

"Perhaps the next time you choose to side against us, you can do me the honor of letting me know."

   Up in the tree, Mary turned her head and glanced up, glanced away.

   "If it serves the Society to do so," she sent, mind-to-mind.

   Mary turned her face to the sun, closed her eyes. She let the warmth of the rays soothe her.

   The 64 Comet was parked in the small lot of Rydel Ridge. Matthew was sitting on the hood, leaning back on the windshield, eyes closed.

   He was taking in the same sun as young Mary.

   End Episode One...

www.ingramcontent.com/pod-product-compliance
Lightning Source LLC
Chambersburg PA
CBHW051831170626
46807CB00003B/1120